GW01401368

Dark Country: Book One

Dark Country: Book One, Volume 1

Bobbydale

Published by Bobbydale, 2024.

DARK COUNTRY: BOOK ONE

First edition. December 2, 2024.

Copyright © 2024 Bobbydale.

ISBN: 979-8230915140

Written by Bobbydale.

"Life is often an unspoken experience, enjoy it and learn from it, in the end, it'll help you."

Chapter 1

Clop!

A log split in two, one of the pieces picked up and placed on the chopping block. A quiet man clad in plain creamy tanned leather clothes. Grasped the axes shaft, rising it above his head. Bringing it down with some effort.

Clop!

Chimes jingled, clicked, and clopped against bone and wood. Tied by hair and fiber string.

Once an outlaw, the man had found that he'd prefer his days in the small clearing. The trees rustling just beyond with fall colors.

He set the axe down. Listening to the chimes move from the breeze. Glancing at the symbols and webs situated amongst them. They hung on the edge of his roofed porch.

His rocking chair creaked in the breeze. He glanced away at the quiet forest in contemplation.

Setting his Axe aside, he gathered the wood split into almost sheets. Carrying it into his cabin. The sun was gathering near the horizon, it would soon be dark, perhaps within a few hours.

He set the wood next to the wood stove, before grasping a meduim bucket, a pale for water.

He carried it down the stairs and towards the well just off bout twenty paces. The well had a manual water pump, he placed the pale down under the faucet.

Pumping the handle slowly as he listened to the terribly quiet forest. He faltered in his task, he heard a faint rumble. Staring at the water spilling out of the faucet. He expressed a sign quietly.

Taking the pale of water back to his cabin. Setting it aside near a basin and the wood stove.

He moved back towards the chopping block just to the left of his entry onto the porch. He didn't leave the porch, turning where he set the axe down.

Taking it inside to put away.

The rumble grew, a backdrop of sound compared to the forest that bristled in branches, in sticks.

He grasped his long rifle, carefully chambering a few rounds. The rumble became distinguishable. Horses, someone was coming.

He expected as much, Outlaw wasn't in a hurry, making himself the last of his brewed tea. The embers in the wood stove still warming the pot.

He added a hint of honey and crushed leaves. Taking his metal cup outside to set it on the little table near his rocking chair.

He closed his door, taking a seat in his rocking chair with a long rifle laying in his lap.

The horses, or say the horsemen didn't take long to break into the clearing. The clopping of horses slowing to a walk after breaking out of the forest. Though as if expecting their reactions.

They looked weirded out, the clearing of his abode chilled their hearts a little. Chimes hung on the trees at the edge of the clearing. Spanning into the trees In a circle.

Not just a thin line, but rather a few meters of tree were covered in them.

It was a creepy sight, there were five of them. Cowboys, dressed in them lawful forces in the city. Outlaw suspected they were looking for someone. They were traveling light, aside from the expected firepower.

When they saw the cabin, there was a quiet talk amongst them before inevitably spotting him in the shadowed porch.

There was more discussion before they began to dismount. The seeming leader of the five making his way up the beaten path.

"Howdy sir!"

He greeted, Outlaw tipped his hat.

"Howdy, what can I do you lads for?"

Outlaw said returning the greeting.

A warm smile spread across the leaders face.

"We are lookin for a woman, twenty years of age. Heard she was kidnapped in these parts. You outta know something bout that?"

Outlaw shook his head after a moment of thought.

"Can't say I have, sir. Don't much see people in these parts. If she out there it ain't near here."

The man tsked, the answer was worrying. She's been missing for only a few days, even still it should be easy to hear stuff out here. These forest, they were way too quiet. You'd expect there to be alot of noise.

But that's not how that went. It was creepy.

"Alright, well sir, mind if me and my boys stay here a night?"

Outlaw nodded.

"Course sir, but I outta warn you to follow the rules, if you'd be kind to do so sir."

The leader tipped his hat.

"Name 'em"

Outlaw nodded, glancing past the cowboy.

"Sir, never have you or your boys walk alone, stick to pairs if your going anywhere."

Hmm?

"Their are some chimes in some of my trees, in the clearin take some and hang them around your encampment, before going to bed."

The Cowboys furrowed his brows. Weirded by the man's rules. But he wasn't done speaking.

"Sir, if ya hear something ignore it. If you can't go in pairs. I'd only ask sir to say one night. Anymore may not be good for sir's men."

The Outlaw said causally. He stood up slowly he did drink some tea, before they arrived, but he saw the colors of the setting sun. It was time to head in.

"That all the rules?"

Mm, the Outlaw nodded.

"Yes Sir, I won't be available till sunrise. If ya need water there is a well over yonder. Not hard to locate. If you'll excuse me sir."

The leader nodded watching the man step into his cabin and closing the door. He heard a slow bolt.

Hmm.. he glanced at the rocking chair, before turning away and waving to his men. "We set up camp here. Roger go gather some chimes from the trees in the clearing. Tyler, go with him. Stick together."

He expressed the rules. Without much elaborating on them.

There were naturally weird looks, but they followed.

Chapter 2

They made camp, hanging chimes as the sun slowly fell. It's light no longer reaching the grass, instead shadowing the ground of the clearing now.

Out of the five, there was Roger, a short stout man. His looked matted, he wore some red bold colors. His bandana, shirt and gun belt had some red too.

Tyler, was a strongman. Wearing more subtle colors, some dark green and some black. His clothing had clean edges, mostly tattered clothing.

Yeniver, a meduimish guy wore the same leather most happen to wear. He did quite agree with traveling how he looked. Having a map, compass, trinkets and survival tools.

Then there was Leeroy, wearing a full sheriff uniform, he was an average guy, but where he looked average. His skills as a sharpshooter outta be the best in the county.

Finally, their leader Johnathan. He was the leading search party. He had similar uniform, with grayer colors. He led this search party after the towns mayor expressed his worry. Apparently some bandits were using the forest to kidnap folks.

Unfortunately the man's daughter was a victim this time.

So naturally they were dispatched personally.

They have been looking, but there was something wrong with the forest. Like looking at a still pond when it was windy out.

The only real sound they heard were the bristling trees, on the stretch of road they were riding. They only crossed one branching path. Which led them here.

To this clearing surrounded by chimes. Like protection. He didn't agree with the weird man in the cabin or the chimes that held a creepy significance to the man.

But he outta mostly follow the rules. Though he suspected they could part with some of those rules.

What could possibly go wrong? They are the only ones really out here.

He shook his head, regretting asking to stay a night. The chimes were way too fuckin creepy.

Maybe the man in the cabin did know something, maybe he is a murderer or something that makes these chimes for some bullshit reason.

He didn't much understand the almost cold shoulder given by the man in the cabin. Just didn't make since.

He put it out of mind. Yeniver got up "I gotta go take a piss."

Roger smirked. "Want company?"

Yeniver clicked his tongue. "Fuck Off"

Roger laughed

Yeniver sniffled, walking near to the end of the clearing.

Chimes with a creepy look clicked off each other giving a hollow bone knock. He scoffed muttering about the creepiness and sneering at the superstitious man in the cabin. What could chimes do?

Spread a creepy atomsphere, sure. But protect? Against what? Ghost? Demons. Yea right fuck off with that shit.

Roger and Tyler gathered fire wood. Making a place for a fire pit. The sun had set and they were working off some oil lamps.

Eventually Yeniver stumbled back.

"Encounter anything, tough guy?"

Yeniver shook his head. "Nope just chimes.. they really creep me out. We should destroy them"

Johnathan squinted his eyes. "I don't think we should do that. Regardless of how absurd the idea of they are. We should at least respect the Mr and his rules a little bit."

Yeniver shivered. "Well I ain't hanging those things near me. Fuck that shit."

Johnathan shrugged. "You do you."

They got the fire started. Listening to the crackles talking about some small issues or worth conversations.

"You folks believe in them ghost and demons them natives believe in?"

Yeniver nodded. "A little"

Roger laughed. "Not a cent of care for it to be honest. Never seen these things before so I doubt they'd exist. Them natives just high off their rockers."

Johnathan nodded slowly. "Your right. I've been in forest plenty, aside form this place. I've never really stumbled on weird stuff. I mean i've heard stories, and i've seen some oddities. But nothin that can't be explained easy."

The conversation eventually died down. The fire had the same thought. And eventually they retired to bed.

In the cabin.

Outlaw stoked the fire quietly. Chimes hanging from the beams above him.

He was a quiet man. Preferring to sticking to his own devices. Yet his head raised and he glanced up for only a moment.

The chimes.. were clicking together softly. His eyes twitched and he expressed himself. "mm.."

The night weared on. And eventually even Outlaw turned in for the night.

It's was a peaceful night.

Chapter 3

Outlaw opened his eyes. Light of the suns rays beaming into his cabin. Getting up, he makes him some herbal tea, washes his face. Then unbolts the door. Grasping his long rifle he steps out. The three men were still sleeping. So he sat down in his rocking chair and quietly listened.

Not long after, his guest woke up, their fireplace embers. It was only after an hour that he saw their leader, Johnathan. Make his way up the path.

"Mornin, say there are five of us. You seen two men since yer wakin sir?"

Outlaw frowned at his words. "Not since yesterday. Did you follow the rules?"

Johnathan made a slight face, but nodded.

"Course sir, maybe they went for a piss."

Outlaw grunted. "Hopefully that's the case, pardon my coldness yesterday. Strangers in these parts aren't one for trustin, never know if you got bandits or travellers."

Johnathan smiled lightly at him

"No harm done, I'll get goin now. Outta find out where them two went before we leave."

Outlaw nodded. "just be out of here by mid day sir, this place is an unkind beast, I'd hate to see ya turning back if you can't escape it."

He was sincere, but this cowboy didn't take his words to heart. Contributing it to the world's of a paranoid feller.

He didn't much care if they believed him or not, as long as they followed the rules he wouldn't have any issue with them.

However two went missing? At night? During their rest from the sounds too. That sounded awfully like somebody broke the rules.

He wasn't privy to the order, nor felt asking. As long as they left, before it was too late. They'd save themselves, he knew they could.

The trio traced the clearing and he eventually saw them dip into the trees. Standing up he decisively shut his door, bolting it.

Opting to spend his day inside. He pulled away the hide rug, underneath a cellar door. He keeps his foods, fermented beverages and dried meats.

With the chill of winter on its way, he felt that a nice stew was in order. So he set to pulling out respective ingredients from down under.

Outlaw quite enjoyed the quiet life. It has its dangers, it had its positives. It connected him to the land, to its culture, he naturally chose to embrace it.

Despite the risk, one of the reasons he didn't much agree with city life was the absence of these things. Not much in the way of wild life, flora. It left things to be unsaid, a bustle of constant interaction and concepts too saturated.

Just wasn't his cup of tea.

Another reason he didn't much agree with it, was the disregard of another's belief, or the alienation of not taking advice in one's land.

Even if it told to do so.

These guests, he allowed in his clearing were great examples of that. The chimes weren't just protection charms, they were signs of respect to the land, they were quiet warnings to him, they were there to keep his mind at peace. They were for communication to them. The creatures out there. The peoples out there.

He did have some dream catchers. They were protections, but perhaps not in the way these men so blatantly thought.

It was none of his business. But he truly hoped they respected his land, as he respected it.

There were troubles, if one weren't so kind to it. If they broke the rules, they disrespected them. Some call them spirits, others local deities. He didnt have a real name for them, opting to call them.. well them.

The trio. Johnathan, Tyler and Leeroy had skirted the clearing edge. Faltering at a place where the chimes break away.

Or rather were some were broken and others damaged. A few beyond the passage were still, some of their strings snapped, cut.

They glanced at each other, noticing tracks through there.

"What the-" Tyler started. Johnathan grimaced. "Let's hurry"

There was blood on some of the bark of the trees.

So they hurried, worried by what could have happened to Roger and Yeniver.

They may have rushed out, but even a mile into the forest showcased no manner of clue.

Two miles, three, four even. They looked, sticking together. Found nothing, their worry grew. Then they saw something.

At the base of a tree the found the bloody remains of a woman. She was severely decayed as if she has been out here for weeks. Oddly she looked somewhat intact for a corpse in the forest.

Chapter 4

No nibbles, no bugs. No animals. No flies.. Nothing.

What's worse? Her chest was caved in, her jaw missing and there was signs she was originally in the trees. Looking up they could see old weird robe like black wires. they seemed snapped?

It scared them and they back tracked. Looking into the trees with harsh worry.

"I think that fuckin native man in the cabin did this to her. That sick man!"

Johnathan could not retort. However he did somewhat agree.

"Lets confront him"

When they broke back into the clearing they were thrown off guard. The sun, it was almost mid day! There is no way over eight hours have passed!

Johnathan blinked at it, but assumed they had time.

He waved at Tyler and Leeroy as he drew his revolver. They both drew theirs.

Outlaw was in the midst of making stew when he heard an almost banging knock.

"We know yer in there you sick fuck! Open up!"

What? He looked confused, Grabbing his long rifle.

Bang! Bang! Bang!

Louder thuds of knocks.

"Open up or we will force our way in!"

Outlaw stood up slowly raising his rifle toward the door. This was one of the issues with guest and why he only allowed them to stay a day.

If they didnt follow the rules, if they didnt leave by mid day.. whos to say they wouldnt start thinking the wrong ideas.

"I'd highly advise you not to do that."

He said moving so he wouldn't be directly in front of the door. If they started firin things'll get messy.

"We know you killed that woman and took our men!"

He frowned at their assumptions. "And why would i have any reason to do so sir?"

"For your sick rituals you nat-"

Outlaw interrupted him. "Sir, I am of no tribe nor a skinwalker of dark medicine. I have no reason to take your people or touch another person. You broke the rules and now they are after you. This is no longer my place to handle, but theirs!"

He said adamantly. Infact Outlaw wasn't apart of a native tribe. He may have had some of their culture. But that didn't aquant to being associated with them.

Whats more the blatant racism against the natives. He knew quite a few and to express that they commit these evils was a serious crime in his books.

A heinous accusation he wouldn't take lying down.

So he finalized his stance.

"I don't welcome you here any longer. Your aversion to the native and their lands is a reminder why I hate you city folk! Take your horses and ride your own passage!"

He didn't hear anything after. Only his breath, then..

"We will be back with a larger party to charge you. Your a wanted man!"

WIth loud footsteps he heard them step off his porch. He sat down again. It be wise to wait till morning. So he stirred the pot some more and prepared for a long day.

He was glad they didn't take it too far, they could have tried the windows, but his windows were blocked by wooden cages and barbed wiring.

Seems like things'll heat up a little.

He wasn't looking forward to it.

Galloping horses roared down the path, three riders the trio from before looked flushed, there was a strange look in their eyes. Back at the cabin before they left. aside from the man in the cabin talking they heard strange cries, felt watched and goosebumps rise.

Like being stared at by a predator. they shivered, each time they knocked. The things.. the.. beast? No it was hard to depict them.

They seemed to grow numerous. So the trio left in a hurry. Terrified, Johnathan told the man in the cabin those empty words. A promise that could hold water if they get out alive.

He grimaced at the feelings he had. And spurred his horse on faster.

His men felt the same way, but they couldn't help but be taken aback at the sights around them.

Their in the trees..

Corpses swaying in the branches, hanging and dangling. Amongst them. Roger and Yeniver.

Chapter 5

The night was quiet and peaceful, he slept In nicely. When the suns rays bathed him in golden light. Did he get up and wash up. He carefully unbolted the door. Having already grasped his long rifle.

Stepping outside the clearing was quiet with the exception of a few left horses.

He sat on the porch for a while. But the morning wore on without issue. After eating he set out to check the damage. To see what they did. Whom and why they angered them.

He checked the campsite first.

An old pit, beaten grass Where they laid their beds. Near two of the spots. Where their equipment actually still lay.. odd.

He saw missing chimes, never set up.

He had an expression, this was the first broken rule no?

He then checked along the clearing edge. Stopping short of a disturbed area of chimes. To his shock, damaged, broken twine, bones smashed and sticks scattered, then wire hanging and cut.

He felt anger at this. No.. this was where it started. Then they ignored the chimes. Or at least the missing did.

He stared further into the disturbed area. Where he saw dried blood on the bark of a tree. He threw his lone rifle over his shoulder, a strap of robe holding it to his back, before pressing into the forest.

Unlike them city folk, he could move with almost ease. He saw the signs sooner. Finding himself in front of a corpse. A woman, she appeared greatly decayed.

He crouched in front of her. She had a bloodied and broken stark white chime in her hands.

They were quite hostile when chimes were messed with. It didn't seem to warrant the deaths. But he assumed there was a reason.

He glanced up, backpedalling to get a good view.

Black wire, no.. that's not wire. That's hair, black strands of hair, woven into robe and used to hang.

Hmm..

On his way back to the cabin, Outlaw gathered the bones of small animals, sticks and fiber twine. He even plucked some stones, acorns and shells from dead snails.

the forest, though quiet, was peaceful, in fact it was actually too quiet, but oftentimes the activity in the forest of this area was dictated by the season. In winter, it'll be desolate.

On his way back he stumbled on a dear skull, implanted in the base of a tree. He paid little mind, but noticed the inherent lack of bones outside of that.

Something to consider over jerky and elderberry wine.

Back at the cabin He opted to spent the rest of the day crafting new chimes. bolting his door at night, sleeping, waking and continuing the process after some breakfast.

The days were nice, listening to the chimes sway and knock together. To the occasional whistle of birds flying south for the coming winter and the breeze of the cool fall days.

Chimes were of great spiritual importance and respect. So he spent a great deal of his last fall days on creating them. Slowly, and with steady hands.

There was a sort of bliss to it.

When he had finished he went ahead and cleared up the broken chimes. Hanging new ones with a strange feeling of eyes on him. Not hostile, but rather an approving stare, he smiled lightly.

Moving as he checked up on chimes and hung new ones. When heading back to his cabin a breeze blew in, colder than before.

The winter chill had arrived. He looked up at the partially clouded skies and reckoned it was time to make the trips. He decided he will depart tomorrow at noon.

Nodding at this he went ahead and cleaned his cabin out for the coming days.

Sweeping out dust, cleaning the wood stove out of ash. Arranging furniture so it makes as much room as he can afford.

When the sun began to set he prepared a large pot of stew.

Setting out a three bowls.

Outlaw opened his door, allowing the dying light into the cabin. He made sure the door would remain open. Using the head of his Ax to keep it so.

He then pulled the hide rug aside, opening his cellar, climbing down and lit a small oil lamp.

Showcasing a few shelves of goods. He grabbed a hide backpack, storing these goods into it carefully.

He then wrapped a wooden closed container. He climbed up the ladder. Placed his backpack aside and climbed back down to grasp a few wooden jars.

His finger ran across the jars slowly, faltering when he heard footsteps on his porch.

Mm, he grapped a wooden jar at the end a soot of dried sap smeared into it. Then he climbed the ladder again.

Taking note of two silhouettes, in the doorway, beyond them the night had begun to show its colors.

Outlaw didn't mind these two, closing his cellar he moved the items away to his table, before moving the rug back. The stew was still simmering; he didn't acknowledge the two, but knew well enough they were there.

Outlaw sat down near the stove, removing the lid he filled two bowls. Turning to find the soundless silhouettes standing hardly a few feet from him.

He handed them the bowls. Whom passed the second to the second figure. These were them. Yes, the ones in the forest. These were a part of them. It's difficult to express them.

They looked similar to bushmen, or guily men, but he only paid enough attention to their overall vague figures.

Outlaw wasn't stupid enough to focus on their heads, nor any other part of them.

He only acknowledged the fact they were there and they were to join him for his last day here till next spring.

He supposed it was another respect. But straightforward. It's often taboo to interact with them, perhaps that was the case amongst the native tribes, but he had long broken that taboo.

Though it may differ between tribes and cultures. He went off his own interpretation. He hadnt had a terrible experience, but certainly understood the issue of disrespecting them.

The spirits, or them. Were very hostile if disrespected greatly. He had seen a few unfortunate souls die at their hands.

Another issue to be mindful of is, some of these, creatures were sinister. Like the second figure, he felt a chill glancing at it. Not a winter chill, but one of prickled goosebumps. Like there was something wrong with it. He deduced that more than likely, it was a skinwalker.

Wether it had bad intentions, he could never figure out. It would explain the less than peaceful days in the forest at night.

Anywho, Outlaw didn't grab himself a bowl. He had other plans. With water warming on the stove he took his shirt off. Then grasped the wooden jar. Within was an ash paint. Made of ash from grounded charcoal and cremated animal. Animal fat, and finally a sap substance.

He used warm water to mix the paint. Slowly stirring it with his finger.

One of the rituals outlaw practices.

He has lived a long time on this land. He has seen events that no longer scare him, he still practices this a protection of sorts.

He applied the body paint slowly. The sound in the cabin is almost soundlessly deafening. Except his breath, the crackling embers, and the footsteps.

They left, he kept a grim look about him. Things went smoothly, as they have before, But these sorts of occasions weren't happy for him.

Though difficult to articulate his emotion. He had settled on being 'used' to it, aware of it.

Chapter 6

Winter was an evasive chill, a creeping unstoppable cold, the limitations of flame when doused left you with cold chills.

It was in all things, water, ground, air, plant life, animals, everything. A cruel beast it has always been, and always will be.

Outlaw felt creeping chill, cold icy hands reaching across his covers, the cold stinging his cheeks.

Barely quelled by the kindled light of the sun rising. Outlaw signed, he had slept. Not well, but sleep nonetheless. Committing to his routine despite the cold blowing in from the open doorway.

He had breakfast, packed up and took a step out of his open doorway. Inhaling deeply, exhaling slowly.

He took some chimes with him, taking care to hang them on his backpack and didn't neglect taking his long rifle.

He had the body paint across his upper torso, a rite of passage. Though mostly hidden. He couldn't hide the clear markings across his chin, ears, upper cheeks and hands.

Setting out, he stepped on the beaten path, there were two paths. One lead further into the forest the other out of it. This was his path, so he turned and began his trek.

The forest in fall was a distort swirl of branches and decay. Piles of fallen leave hustled, branches swayed. No sing song spoken between them, the birds gone for a time.

His walk was quiet. Except for the creaking rope. The sway of silhouettes in the trees.

Outlaw paused.

He looked up, swaying corpses. They were in the trees. Countless kinds, many dead, many more decayed to the bones, fewer fresh.

Then he saw them, five distinct. Newer, they were the lowest. Hoisted not far into the trees.

He couldn't help but catch his breath.

They were taboo breakers, in this forest the spirits were a sinister force. They were not kind to those whom ignored the warnings, the rules, and them. No respect, in their eyes was forfeiting your life.

Hostile spirits, well he wasn't entirely sure if this was a normal. To him it has been, but. Was it really?

Outlaw could only exhale a sign and continue on.

He has no business asking, it was their fault after all. He had no grievance about their loss of life.

About mid day he saw the edges of the forest, a welcome sign the spirits were kind.

It was hard to articulate the cause, but there was a time where you had to leave the forest. Or be stuck within for a desperate time, waiting for the next day unsure if you'll survive.

This is why he mentioned leaving the forest before midday, they would have gotten out and saved their lives, had they followed.

Breathing through his nose, Outlaw picked up his pace.

The trees thinned, the bodies he saw before nowhere in sight. Before him rolling hills and shallowed plains stretched out. He would soon hit the main road, a day's walk should suffice.

Where the forest held little sound, quite an unnerving factor. The surrounding plains despite the oncoming winter livened up considerably.

He couldn't help but smile this time, taking a moment to enjoy the swaying tall grass of the plains, outcropping of rocks, cactus and signs of animals.

It was... refreshing.

Outlaw set down his backpack a ways off the path. Taking shelter in a pine tree, a quick break. He had taken a swig of his waterskin. To whom he brought three. And chewed on some leftover jerky he packed last night.

He had three destinations.

There was a small community near the base of the mountains, am almost weeks walk. With the rolling hills he couldn't quite see the mountains, but he was sure soon he would when they ebbed out into more flatter plains.

His second location was a tribe he often bartered with in winter. They had something he couldn't just get easily. They were much further than the mountain folk.

That said he was not headed to either of these locations.

The third location and his first pitstop was actually a local lady. They called her "Blood Seer" she was barely a days travel, but he would need to go off the path. there was a lesser known valley deeper in the wider rolling plains.

He would find her there. She was one of his stops for trade and barter.

Outlaw often wouldn't travel near the westerners, their cultures were to alien he supposed. Or at least he wasn't too willing to change for their cities.

So this walk without path wasn't an issue, just another venture where normal man dont walk easy.

He hoisted his backpack on his shoulders and begin delving into the rolling plains, where hills rose and fell slowly.

He had a few hours before sun set, so he had to take it easy. The Seer's land was a cautionary place to tread. So he would prefer to not cross its boundaries at night nor camp near It.

He planned to make camp in an hour.

Chapter 7

The setting sun illuminated the back of outlaw, he stood in an outcrop of tree, ahead by a few miles he spotted signs of boundary markings.

He set his backpack down and begun to set up camp. Hanging the few chimes he brought with him, in this case he did it for extra protection, Outlaw wasn't going to rely solely on his ritual.

Spirits outside where he lived was a different story. Different procedures and taboos existed, Different creatures sinister or not.

He had to play it safe. As someone whom has connection to the spirit world he wouldn't want to attract the wrong attention.

Back home those spirits, Though very dangerous. Were manageable, because he knew how to manage their mutuality.

Yet he never let his guard falter outside of that, a time ago he had done so, and it didn't end so well for him.

Being attacked is certainly unpleasant when its by something you can't easily banish. That's a time he'd prefer to forget. Being perceptive is a talent, and a skill. He wasn't as perceptive or unperturbed as he is now. The difference is, before in that time past. He had help, but now? That help has passed, their ashes reincarnated into the cycle of life.

He stoked a small fox fire. Or well he calls it a fox fire, where one digs a hole deep enough to limit the fires range of light.

This was wild country, where spirits maybe, they were the least of his worries. Rather it were humans he had an issue with.

More so, bandits.

Earlier in the day he had set traps and caught some game. Near the outcropping of trees he skinned and gutted them, taking only the meat he could cook.

The reason to do this away from one's campsite is to not draw predators to it whilst you sleep.

Having a bear, or some other predator stumble across you sleeping, well. That would be an unpleasant waking experience.

Outlaw made sure to harvest the bones and hide. He disdained not using all of the game, but he really couldn't bring this with him. So he only hoped predators or scavengers would find It a nice free snack.

As night came, so did the colder air. Yes, winter was beginning to set in and soon enough a cold front would move in, for now the degrees would degrade, but once the cold really set in, the degrees would drop.

He suspected he had a few days before this front would hit. His thoughts wandered briefly, but eventually Outlaw found himself in a light sleep.

The night went on without a hitch, the landscape was alive with noise. Nothing compared to the springtime, but certainly alive in its own way.

When the sun began to rise, so did Outlaw. He hydrated and ate a snack, before packing up, burying the cinders of the fire pit.

He hoisted his backpack on his shoulders. Checked his gun to make sure the parts worked as they should. He knew the cold could mess with parts, though it wasn't quite time for it.

It's best to be safer than sorry later, starting a habit can be good, before the events of it happening.

He nodded with satisfaction and began his trek towards the boundary.

The blood seer, she is quite the odd ball. But he always found her strange, even scarier than the spirits of the land.

He knows the local tribe near her actaully considers her a skinwalker, he can't say if this is true persay, but he does know some of the acts she commits are certainly labeled evil. Some of the more sinister spirits are bound to her.

At least that is what he noticed in the years visiting her hidden place.

The boundaries were strange, almost wicked. They deterred more than immaterials but also any human. Or most who found the boundary off putting, like an omen made manifest.

The Blood Seer was ruthless when it came to settling her territory. In at least this part he saw the bones of animals painted, even a few suspicious chimes that looked wicked at first glance. He made sure not to be near those.

Despite trading with the Blood Seer, he had to be mindful of the places in her territory. Given she is a dark shaman, the name should be enough to express the issue of crossing into their territory.

Weirdly beyond the boundary, it was dead silent, the shadows elongated, he spotted the same markings, but larger and they were paintings. He assumed they were curses and rightfully avoided them. There was a beaten path, but it was unnaturally devoid of movement.

Not even the grass here swayed, even when there was a breeze, and the breeze whispered.

He did not listen, and soon enough an hour of walking yielded him results. He saw the semblance of a large pseudo tent, wrapped by wood and given a weird structural shape.

He approached with caution. Noticing somebody within. So he called out.

"Blood Seer?"

The figure paused. They uttered in a gravel voice.

"I's not de Seer, she's within furthers"

Outlaw nodded to the figure.

"Thank you, this one shall pardon himself"

The figure did not respond, moving back to their task, from here he could smell the heavy metallic scent.

Blood.

Moving away he continued his journey. He did know this territory was home to some other figures. To save himself the trouble he often didn't update himself on the territory's dealings nor lightly interacted without reason.

The upside is, these figures were aware of him. Had they not been. He wouldn't have gotten so far without being hunted and used. It didn't take long to see her dwelling. The trees here gnarled, wicked chimes hanging from their decayed branches.

There was a large rounded building, or well a shabby-made of wood and cloth. Akin to a tent if anything.

He could feel the eerie oppression here, there were many things, but he paid no mind to them. He was not a dark shaman, he didn't want to see that knowledge.

He said again.

"Blood Seer?"

There was not a sound, but the silence was broken.

"Oh Outlaw? Yes yes, your Outlaw."

She said, always able to startle him. She had been following him for a time.

He watched her bypass him without a sound of her footsteps. She turned back.

"Come, inside. We's, speaks on deal, yes?"

such an odd ball.

Chapter 8

Blood Seer may have been an odd ball in speech, but her appearance was very unkind to look on and unpleasant to be in the presence of.

The Blood Seer is an old woman, draped in a black cloak woven like a net, her attire tinged with dark, greenish hues.

She wears a deer skull over her head, its antlers adorned with dark chimes, small skulls, and black feathers. A bloody handprint, dried and dark red, stains the skull, with a few streaks still visible.

Her arms are covered in tattoos resembling spider webs, and her hands are decorated with red beads, netting, and sharp bits of metal. She moves with an eerie, ethereal grace, with such an odd ball speech pattern.

He wouldn't say this to her out loud, in mild fear of being turned into a festive stew. He did not know if her or her followers were cannibals, but he would not want to find out first hand.

Outlaw followed her inside. The entrance is draped with layers of faded fabric, fluttering slightly in the wind.

Inside, the air is thick with the scent of earth and herbs, mingling with something darker. The ground is covered in a mix of worn animal pelts and dried grasses, giving the place an earthy, grounded feel.

He smiled at that lightly, He agreed with the feeling.

Herbs hang in bundles from the low ceiling, some familiar, others strange and twisted. Around the edges of the tent, shelves made from rough-hewn wood hold jars filled with mysterious ingredients, alongside various ritual tools and small effigies.

Though Outlaw did understand what certains were used for, some others looked sinister to him, even if they truly werent.

At the center of the space, a low, round table sits surrounded by stone altars, each marked with offerings. A fire pit in one corner glows with embers, casting flickering shadows that dance across the space. Over the fire hangs a blackened cauldron, simmering quietly.

He glanced at the space, that same feeling came back. Almost like being home, but here there was no mistake that there was something unsettling. He didn't dwell on it long and took his backpack off to retrieve the items.

Outlaw actually made some of the ingredients the Blood Seer uses. He carefully took out two small wooden jars and a doll.

when She saw them her eyes lit up. She remarked as he handed then over carefully.

"Outlaw, yous always braves to handle these crafts.. you say your no shaman, but these.. they say otherwise you knows?"

She wasn't wrong, the three items in question were meant for dark rituals. The fact he wasn't someone who used that kind of magic should be perplexing.

The Blood Seer had received, a doll.

A small doll crafted from twisted roots and sinew, stuffed with hair and nails taken from a corpse found in a haunted forest. Given he lives in a weird forest, she knew of it as she did visit him once..

She was surprised he found and harvested corpses.

The doll is wrapped in strips of animal hide marked with blackened runes, using soot from a fire that once consumed a witch's pyre.

Unless he had other connections this shouldn't be an easy item to craft. If he isn't a dark shaman than he is something else. She just couldn't understand his dislike when he does these things.. ha..

She looked at the other items. One of them is called bloodroot ink. A crimson ink, made from the sap of a bloodroot, mixed with ash of burned bones from.. a cursed burial ground..

She gave Outlaw a hard look.

"Yous sure yes? You be a good student to show!"

Outlaw gave her a look. "I must humbly decline the Blood Seer"

She waved at him in annoyed dismissal looking at the final item even tasting it.

It was a salve. Thick black ointment, tasted like raven.. ah. It's shadow salve. Made by raven fat, nightshade and-"

She spat the ointment out. She forgot about nightshade. There was a worser indegredent, instill born animal crushed and grinded bones! She could taste it.

Bah she did not mind it. Instead she gave Outlaw her end of the bargain.

A ritual dagger, heavily cursed. Bound by spirit, drenched. It had all the qualities. By what means He needed this she did not question. No longer caring.

Outlaw carefully examined it. Even whilst his skin prickled by its curse. "Thank you, this'll work nicely."

She gave him a look as if he was contradicting her words a moment ago. But she shooed him.

"Okay, okay, go shoo, i's wants to bind spirit now!"

Outlaw nodded and swiftly left without another word. He didn't want to be around for it.

On his passage out, his skin felt hot, he saw three figures, they were in the corner of his sight and looked off put, he did not glance at them. Deciding that he needed to leave now.

The heat was his body paint reacting.

Chapter 9

Outlaw was a brave man to explore and trade with unkind forces. But he wasnt brave enough to stay and watch.

He would consider himself alive for those reasons. There are times to be brave, and there are times to not be brave. Its a balance of its own. Just as to be smart and not be killed.

He only meld with these forces for greater and better trades, he did this for his own survival back at home.

But now it was time to get away and out. The Blood Seer's territory was a terrible beacon, he didnt want to be in it too long, less he attract the wrong crowd.

His protections spanned as far as he walked his destinations, nothing more nothing less. If he stayed here.

He would be exposed.

In the same hours it took to arrive was the same to leave.

The sun had only taken barely a quarter into the sky. It was still morning, almost noonish. He departed soon after, not opting to rest here. He decided to reach the road before nightfall. there is a settlement a days off, he could use it despite his dislike.

He knew of a shopkeeper there who would allow him to restock.

So that was his destination or a pitstop on his way.

as He traversed back he stopped by his last encampment to rest for a moment.

He scoped out his spyglass. Because of the landscape one could see for miles. So it wasn't hard to spot black dots moving ahead.

He couldn't tell from this distance what they were so he kept caution when he began to move, the dots had moved behind some coverage so he lost track of them.

He took his long rifle off his back, taking a gander to see if it's loaded.

He had a breech rifle, they packed twelve rounds. It's been his trusty friend when things need a few bullets to solve issues.

Especially bandits.

His thoughts were interrupted when he heard a small thunder. A whiz rang past him, hitting his backpack, he dived into the tall grass rolling right, gun pointed forward so it wouldn't clip above the grass and expose him. Speak of the devil, and he shall appear.

Perhaps he should've played a little more caution and taken a different route.

He sat in the grass prone listening, the shot sounded like it came from his left, at an angle. He crawled slowly, stopping randomly to listen for a while.

He heard the grass, heard himself and nothing beyond that.

Outlaw frowned, he was blind, but if he got up he could also be dead or injured. From the looks whomever fired had a long rifle.

Don't get it mixed up, Outlaw only called his rifle a long rifle as its often coined like that. It was actually a breechloader, but the person in question clearly had a precision rifle.. which meant..

He signed, he should've ran instead. They take awhile to load so he could of had time, except then he recalled he saw three black dots where he was walking. Which meant either of the two could have also had the same guns, but he could have played with fire and hoped their aim was bad.

It's too late now, the sun beat down on from above as he crawled slowly. He noticed some rocks ahead. Largish big enough to crouch behind.

He reached them jimmying himself up into a sitting position. He took a gander at this height, if the shooter is left and still is left then. He moved right to try and get a better look.

Outlaw sharply inhaled and fell back as he heard distinctive shots, he saw them for barely a glimpse too.

Three shooters, they had moved right!

The outcry of shot rang and this time he wasn't so lucky, he felt a stinging pain in his arm and shoulder, whilst another chipped the rock where his head had been. He fell back into the grass with a hiss, trying to limit his reactions and voice. He scrambled up and charged their position. Two of them had long rifles, the third as if excepting his move fired again soon after.

Outlaw saw this and scrambled to dive, feeling one shot whiz past then a second nick him and a third whiz past. He hit the deck with a gasp.

He was pinned!

He opted to fire before the other two reloaded, last he saw they were pouring gunpowder into the barrels..

He inhaled jumping up into a stumbling run he stopped momentarily, aiming his rifle.

The bandit whom thought he learned his lesson was momentarily caught off guard. He quickly shuffled to fire back, not before Outlaw steadied his aim and fired, readjusted and fired again!

Outlaw hunts in the hunting seasons with this same rifle, so who's to say he isn't a great shot?

The bandits now take cover, not without some injured though and not without a few more rounds either hitting them or flying past.

Outlaw ducked down and began crawling again to break sight of the bandits. He had fired half his cartridge.

Now he contended with adrenaline and the heat from his wounds.

Adrenaline could both be a great natural medicine, and a terrible curse if you weren't trained or experienced.

One of the major reasons was tunnel vision. Keeping awareness was on one's best priority. Losing it would be unpleasant when it backfires.

He crawled trying to ignore and resist both. He could feel his heartbeat. Strong and fast.

Glancing at the sky, he felt this was going to be a long day.

Chapter 10

Daniel inhaled and exhaled lightly. His brother Trevor reloaded his long rifle. "Fuckin hell, I told ya to aim for the torso, not the fuckin head. Now look at cha, lookin like someone plugged ya full of holes. Danny, ya see him?"

Danny with the breechloader surveyed the feilds. They had seen the man coming from a ways out. Daniel had a spyglass that They got some some fancy sly trader in town. Been used to ambush strangers for some classic dead man's loot.

"Nope he is playing it safe, fuck he might be dead with all em rounds i greeted em with, want me to see?"

Trevor looked at Danny as if the man had two brain cells right now. "Oh sure, bud. Go out there and see if Mr multishot Is dead we will watch yer corpse from over here. So the scavengers don't get cha"

Danny looked at him funny. "Really? Fuck you then. Maybe I will go out there."

Danny said in a sassy tone right back, returning his eyes to the front. The stranger was a precise shot with a multishot. Like he got some hits too. Sure, but.. he was really hoping they crossed a country bumpkin.

Where da fuck did he come from, not even on the roads. The idea of living Where roads don't run just didn't really cross his mind all that much. Sure it must happen, but he really doesn't see it often.

"Danny! Damnit, stop going into fairyland-"

Danny looked towards Trevor when he witnessed Trevor falling back, blood mist spewing out the side of his head.

The life left his eyes and he hit the dirt.

Daniel reacted first.

"Trevor!"

He ignored the pain and picked up his rifle to stand up and fire. He saw him, the fucker had crawled up real close to their position. The first engagement wasn't that far. At least ninety-five meters.

Click

Daniel's face fell.

He had forgotten to reload. He toppled when three shots ripped into him. Danny rose up alongside Daniel, he fired two rounds, but felt the sting when the stranger turned on him in quick succession.

The exchange between Trevor dying, Daniel standing up alongside Danny. Only five seconds had passed.

Danny dropped in pain, he still was alive. Daniel was too, but incapacitated.

Outlaw wasn't doing any better, he had taken another two to his already injured arm. But he did drop the last two. He knelt, ejected the magazine. Noticing he had one round left. He changed out for a new magazine moving with practiced ease.

Or as easy as one could with pain.

He stumbled back to his feet and pushed, opting to move right and coming up from behindish to them.

Good he got two, one bandit was breathing but he didn't appear conscious. However the man with a breech rifle?

Aimed where he thought Outlaw was. Raising the rifle Outlaw fired once, then twice. Ending the bandit, he moved to the unconscious one and popped one in their head. Then he rifled through their pockets, taking things he though valuable and stumbled away.

Gunshots carried, he had to get at least away from this area.

It was hard, he had adrenaline for a short bit, but when it waned the real pain hit. A pulsing in his veins.

He set down camp for the day. Sheltering under a low tree, he dug a small fox hole and painfully started a fire.

Now came the hard part, he took off his shirt and accessed the wounds. The easiest to treat were the through in through. The lesser so easy were the ones that never exited. Outlaw opened his backpack and drew some herbs, yarrow, sage, oak bark, etc.

He spent the day treating himself, dealing with the lesser easy ones and bandaging himself. He used the little fox fire to brew some tea, prepare some herbs and commit a ritual to cleanse himself after the gunfight.

When the sun began to set he doused the fire with dirt and held his gun close. Opting to sleep lightly, he hadn't gone far enough to safely start a fox fire at night.

So he slept in the cold with his cloths serving as his warmth and the tree serving as a wind sheild.

An unpleasant night, but it passed quickly. In the morning he restarted the fox fire and brewed more tea.

The herb he used for the tea is named willow bark, a remedy for pain management and regaining energy. He felt fatigued, tired and weak.

He was lucky to not get hit in the vital areas, but he felt this was not good in the long run of his journey.

Only time would tell, but perhaps he should lay low somewhere when he nears the mountains. The further he could get the better.

Chapter 11

Outlaw stumbled and shambled his way further out, nearer to the road. He decided that it would be best to stay where he was now that he was further out away from the scene. But closer to a place he could hide.

Outlaw dug himself a fox fire, but did not light the sticks gathered. He worked in pain, gathering and binding wood of sticks. Before digging out the floor to make a dip. He used stones to hope to hold the water out should it rain.

He draped the small low to the ground structure partially In hide. At least the section he would sleep. Then he made an effort to set some game traps.

The issue is these actions took far longer, trying his best to limit his movement as to not reopen the wounds. He still had to stitch himself, but the scabbing and herbs worked their magic for the time being.

The sun was barely perceptable as it's last rays vanished and the sky darkened. He shuffled back, lighting the small pile of sticks after sparking flint with iron onto tinder mixed with a slight bit of animal fat and wax he made at home during the spring for such camping occasions.

He had smartly left the middle of his little structure open so the smoke may disperse without choking him. Almost akin to a teekee tint, except much much lower to the ground.

He slept well that night after some brewed willow tea.

Nothing of note really happened, though the fire went out quick the embers remained for hours. Only sapped of their strength in the early hours.

Outlaw awoken in the black. He blinked and listened, the wind whispered, a soft tune without coherent word.

He listened and it sang till the sun began to rise. Only then did he rise too.

His task simple. Check the traps, many hasn't gone off in fact very few had, only some game killed by the simple traps. You'd be surprised what a few sticks and a good heavy stone could do. He skinned the game there taking care to gather its bones, useful organs and meat.

He did not forget the hide.

Bringing it back he observed the barely seen road. It was dead quiet out there. No traffic at that hour.

He went back to his camp. Setting sticks over the top of his temporary home. Where the fires smoke would billow. Heat also rises here, good for smoking food.

He gathered sticks and used a hatchet he brought to grasp thicker woods.

The day was simple and he passed his time by using the bones and his hair to weave very small chimes. He was not aware of the spirits here, but he would pay respects for the time he'd be spending.

Time went on like this. He didn't need much, attempting to rest and only eat when nessessary, he had depleted his water skins though and after a day of his routined task. He fashioned a walking stick to balance him and go look for a creek. He glanced at the landscape, tracing where he thought water to be and started. Ponds were naturally common ish, where as creek between the base of rolling hills often pooled.

An easy method to follow, clearly his target.

Winter was an unforgivable season, his chances would be slimmer the longer it wore on.

He could only count His lucky stars when he noticed a small pond. At the lowest point of the hills.

It wasn't full, rather nearly empty. However that was enough he shambled towards it, filling his water skins he headed back.

He'd have to boil it. The pond was still, no running creek flowed Into It, He didn't want to test his luck. Stagnant water was often more dangerous than running water. Even still, always boil it before you drink it. Kills the bad, keeps the good.

The day went on normally. He did notice the road distantly had some traffic, mostly duo or small groups of riders. He supposed something was happening, those riders looked, uniform.

Often meaning enforcers, mercenaries, bandits which were unlikely to the colors.. or military.

He ducked away from his viewing spot. Opting to not be spotted if that happened to be the case.

He kept to his routine and the next few days aside from growing gradually colder went swell.

On the fourth day he had redressed his wounds. The shallow ones were looking well, whereas the deeper one on his shoulder still had some ways to go.

He did realize an issue with his stay here. The game he caught was much fewer, yesterday he caught a rabbit. He had to use a lot of herbs to get what he needed out of it.

He had a large backpack, made of sewn and hide. Each winter he had supplies for the trip. First aid herbs, salves, and ritual cleansing items.

A few mullti-purpose tools he had hanging from the back pack. Goods and clothes he carried for trade, and other misc items for uses in day to day life.

That said, the herbs he packed in the beginning of fall and set down in the cellar. Were beginning to wane.

He supposed he'd have to restock when he reached the mountain tribe.

Alot of these locations were trade for some items, like chains he would gather from one another trade to another and take the real items he needed. It was a daunting task traversing where either was taboo and where most dared not for what he truly needed.

Outlaw could only sign to himself.

He hoped the healing process would speed up, the rituals helped deeply, yet he couldn't help but feel an obscure omen settling over him.

He should move soon. Set up elsewhere, he can't help but feel like he's being watched.

Ever since spotting those riders those eyes were slow to catch him. So was the feeling. Now he determined it and did not sleep peacefully as he normally did.

Chapter 12

Before morning broke, Outlaw packed up early, scuttling his campsite carefully.

He used that same walking stick and the moons natural light to carefully parse his way the opposite direction of the site and road, opting to go around and hit the road nearer to the city.

Though perhaps he should get a good look first at the happenings.

Unbeknownst to Outlaw his sixth sense had saved him. Three figures encroached on the camp as the sun's rays began to peak over the horizon. Using the temporary shadow that began to ebb away. They pushed up to the encampment.

Careful, they peaked into the recent encampment. Making no loud sound, even after discovering the encampment was scuttled.

They looked at each other one of them stepping out of this small hiding spot and using a sun lantern to blink morse code.

There were a few blinks back. The figure turned to his brothern. And flicked his head, they nodded and the figures receded.

Outlaw took his time, but he did see the town. Though he dared not peak any hills, so he stayed in the creeks that ran between them. When he neared the town he set down his backpack in a tree and made a careful approach. Slow and easy.

There appeared to be a significant force of blue colored men. They carried long rifles, some breech some precision.

He recognized them, they were definitely the US military. Given the bias in towns about natives and his trinkets.

Outlaw felt he would not enter without issue. He deliberated, yes he won't attempt, he will continue his passage, but instead of going by road he will have to take a short cut.

He grimaced at that, slowly receding back as to not draw attention, before he headed back to his bag. Time to hit the rock outcrops, a dangerous shortcut.

Wholly unaware that his actions were being watched, the figures did not pursue him further instead emerging onto the road. They were colored in blue uniform.

They had scouted a rumor, found it's truth and tracked the hurt native.

Now they reported this incident.

The captain in charge listened.

"Sir, we have found a scuttled encampment, somehow the redskin knew we were on to him. We tracked him, he was very much injured, we are unsure by whom."

The captain thought, then he smiled lightly.

"Alright continue your scouting of the area. It doesn't matter if they know we are coming, if the native is a part of a group. If not, mm, all the better."

Outlaw unaware of the plot back in the town. He headed for the mountains, their looming figures of snow capped peaks already chilling his bones by staring at their blizzards. Where clouds consumed and misted their unseen true peaks.

The passage of the shortcut was through a large area of rock croppings. Large boulders that he would need to jump and climb over. He often opted to take the road, because this was a very dangerous terrain to cross alone.

In pairs or groups it's plenty safe with some off chance risk. But alone? You may as well cross rapids by swimming.

He had to take this path though, going around is too far, taking the road runs the risk of encountering an early death.

The out croppings had risk, but they were manageable If he took his time.

The reason he held this thought is, the rock croppings of boulders are tightly knit together, with loose Areas, cracks, crevices. Spaces that if you stumble or fall could easily annoint you a slow death by hunger, dehydration or even animals.

He was aprehensive when he saw them distantly, they were large ish, the size of a settlers house. Some rounded some jagged. If he braved the winter on the mountains he could go around, but as he stated earlier. it would take too long and the dangers on the mountain were much greater. He would prefer to enter the mountain only for a day or two, no more.

The mountain tribe there are hardy people, with good reason. They guard a cursed burial site. That was his destination, to trade for the ability to gain access to that, to gather materials.

There was folklore of the mountain spirits, especially the ones whom hunger. With an insatiable appetite of their kins flesh, with the chill of winter biting at any whom neared them, with warped appearances.

He dare not say their name, the mountain tribe calls them hollow, they had names, many names. He opted for hungers. A reminder of their nature. Sticking to straight and simple words was a go to. They reminded him, kept him safe and he appreciated the system. To never forget what was and what could be. What to avoid, what to acknowledge.

The best idea, the method is to ignore them, and avoid possession.

The croppings are ahead. He grimaces at the natural danger. So he decides to camp outside of them today.

Reduce risk as they say, do so with caution and your chance is higher.

He would listen to that advice.

Chapter 13

That night did not pass so peacefully.

a swirl of thunder, crackling and strong. A swirl of black, deafening without pause, static at the helm, both ahead and in the back of his mind.

Whispered winds blew soft imitated faces, drawn pool under splayed figures of blade and bullet.

cries of a hundred, roar of the cannon few. Thunders of clashing in his blackened veiw.

Distant, rumbling, further from far, just beyond the standing structure laid a battle yet true.

He gasped and echoed a quiet look, finding, leading, speaking to an unpleasant sight ahead. He tried to tell them, say to them. That blood was amonk, they shouted, they screamed and sooner stilled did the outlines become.

From afar a line of smoking scent, powder of metallic, eyes of an unspoken pact, moved with uniform in black. The trees curled at their arrival. Swayed away from their trample, he could only watch in terrible understanding.

Without body, without ability, he watched their final goodbyes, for the spirit has perished under that terrible black ire. Outlaw awoken in a cold sweat, gasping for air.

He felt an omen, a strong foreboding. That dream, it was no nightmare. What has happened? And why?

He feels sorrow jumping to his eyes and for a time, he could only cry. When the sun rose, so did he with a reddened face.

Something very bad had happened and he only hoped what he thought was certainly not truth.

He hoped more that a nightmare had occurred than a dream of true events. The morning light after breakfast he carefully started on the misshapen rounded to jagged boulders. His journey slowed significantly, the sun beating down on him.

Outlaw plagued by the dream focused on not slipping or stepping where he shouldn't.

The dangerous terrain was harsh, even carefully he had some unbalanced moments, but no accidents, Outlaw managed past the terrain, coming across the unlucky ones, Remains in deceptive places where it looked easy to escape.

He would not make their mistake, and soon enough he found himself landing on a beaten path near the rock outcropping. He took a moment to situate himself and eat some jerky.

He was half a days travel from his location.

Turning his gaze on the looming mountain, he was headed for the mountain tribe. He could already see their structures carved into the mountain side.

They were a mostly stationary tribe. They did have roamers, but mostly guarding the entrance to the accursed place had been their purpose.

He never did find out the exact reasons for why, or at least why the proximity was so close to the cursed place.

Outlaw had asked before, but doing so felt strained. So he had recanted which seem to lessen that tension. Even if he needs to go and use the burial grounds. They were not easy to get along with or manage to get trust in.

They were not kind to spirit walkers, and they treated him akin to one. Even sometimes going further and naming him a shaman of shadow or the shadow of the forest.

He did not much enjoy these terms as he wasnt apart of any tribe nor held the same standards of their taboos or culture. So he wasn't sure entirely why they referred him to these names.

He does not feel like he is a bad man, practicing dark arts. Nor was he of the insidious or the forest unkind spirits.

The most atrocious name they have sometimes given him is like the ones they give to the spirits of the burial ground. Hollow.

He shook his head, opting to not think further on this topic. Having been walking for a little bit the mountains chill breezed, welcoming him to its cold and harsh sights.

The mountain has some trees, but mostly rock with very little grass. It took a while but he saw the first few of the mountain tribe, he would call them by their true name, of their tribe. But they had refused to give the name and opted for what he had been calling them.

Perplexing and strange? Yes, very.

It was not long until they saw him. Sooner still did a group of them approach.

"Forest shadow you come again for the accursed?"

Outlaw nodded

"Yes yes, restocking for next fall."

They gave him off putting looks, always quite unsettling, but he could never place their looks. The emotions they wore in their eyes and expressions never made sense.

"Be quick, winters chill. The hollows active more so this time."

He frowned at that, dealing with the hollows was always tricky business. The Hungers, he had to be mindful of them.

"I will keep that in mind, I have your items."

He said, but before he could pull his backpack off they waved at him.

"We not want this time, Just be quick and gone by moonrise."

He made a face, but eventually lowered his hands.

"Okay, I will be quick"

Outlaw said, already being led around to the edges of their tribe. They never let outsiders through their town, he is no exception. He is treated with omen, like a dark cloud. A chill to them, he clicked his tongue.

The truth of his dreams didn't lay here. A welcome sign despite their harshness, Which he opted to be understanding of.

The worry of where this dream is at, if at all, is quite high.

He pushed the thoughts aside as he felt goosebumps prick his skin. Deliberately Ignoring by whom caused it, taking advise said not long ago and following it. For ignorance here is a welcome bliss to the dangers of the burial ground, cursed as It is.

Chapter 14

Outlaw was privy to alot, and the mountain tales were certainly something he encountered alot and had mistakenly seen.

Their names were taboo here to speak and that's why he used their hollow, or his hungers terminology. That said, he was here for a few items. Cursed bones, raven feathers and a few herbs that are well known to grow in these places.

As he scoured the grounds he saw figures, emaciated, long and though he saw them indirectly they weren't pleasant. To know they were there.. just waiting to be seen.

A game of madness he would never allow himself.

All these items he gathered was for his final stop, a tribe out by three maybe two days of he pushed it. They were fine, at least on the surface. He actually never knew what they do with the items. Nor did he want to, his friends in the tribe also never spoke to him about it.

When he bundled the herbs with cord, he paused. His head tilting as he picked up on a faint sound, the whimper of a dog?

It came from deeper in the mountains. He wouldn't fall for that, it could of course be an actual dog. That did cross his mind, but it's difficult to take that risk when the hungers could mimic voices.

He heard the whimper again after he stowed the items in question. The whimper was so much closer, and he couldn't help but glance up. A searing chill rippled down his spine. There was a dog, a hound. It had sounded much further away, but now? He could see it.

The hound was fifty paces out. It whimpered, but there was no reason he could see for it.

He hoisted his backpack onto his shoulders, standing slowly as his eyes roved the dog. Black coat largish and with beady eyes.

Nothing appeared immediately wrong, but if that had been the case then he wouldn't have felt that searing chill, nor the right of passage reacting strongly.

How would he react to this?

Something Outlaw himself was figuring out. Eventually the rite of passage cooled and the dog trotted up to him seeming completely normal. It nudged it's head against his leg looking for pettings..

He knelt down to pet it, still investigating. Nothing seemed wrong, acted normal and seemed fine. He chuckled to himself lightly, he had thought he was dealing with a large issue. He patted the dog and decided this was enough and he would head back to let the mountain folk know he was on his way out.

The dog followed for a while but spooked off once nearing the mountain village. He couldn't blame it, the place did give off some airs.

When they saw him coming he was quick about It.

"I have what I need, I leave now."

The warriors who met up with him raised an eyebrow.

"That fast? Not even hour."

Outlaw smiled

"I not need much. Not big demand this winter."

The warriors made an 'ah' face then waved him along to a path that skirts their village from the otherside but allows him to bypass a considerable level of rock outcroppings and dense forest.

"Next year then."

Outlaw nodded.

"Yes, next year."

He started on his way, noting the day he felt he could likely reach River Creek by sunset.

He nodded to himself enthusiastically and set to the path, moving with a slight brisk to his step, his mood unsoured by the feeling of being watched.

The passage he walked ran along a narrow cliff, tall cliff, that degraded until it leveled with the ground where a beaten path break away into some cleared trees and eventually into a line covering of trees that shadowed the path.

He could tell it was a well used path, which explains the maintenance of its wild growths. A slight level of landscaping, here he saw markings on the trees, deep gorges. Like a bear? Hard to say.

Outlaw slowed to give them a passing glance, but eventually carried on, speeding up to a brisk pace. Bears was not a beast he wanted to tackle, they were strong and he felt with his injuries, he would not win.

Luckily he did not encounter a bear, only bones of animals with matted torn furs that loosely draped their bones. He grimaced at the scenes last he checked, bears don't hunt for sport.

There was so signs of feasting, of course it's hard to tell when it's skin and bones, but the corpses or remains he found had large tears where claws raked. But no large opening where a bear may eat into the creature.

Outlaw kept walking not wanting to stay here any longer, it may have been a while, but a while didn't mean whatever did that moved on. He only hoped if it was a bear, that it was slumbering somewhere for winter.

If it was a bear.

To his relief, not long after he heard the faint trickle of water, sighting ahead River Creek.

It's called that because there are multiple creeks that slowly bleed into it and you see them, all of them. Like a branching tree, the main creek was large, easily twenty paced wide and was roughly four-ish feet deep.

Outlaw laughed when he saw the creek, having been so tense for several days that this is one of those more reprieving moments. He scouted it's banks and found a good hidden spot, sliding into the indent that was hidden by trees he set his backpack down and sat down.

He listened to the water trickling, relaxing if only for a moment.

Chapter 15

Outlaw enjoyed the creeks peacefulness. Listening to the whispering wind. Although there was a deep lack of other sounds like crickets or any signs of animals. He wasn't too parsed about it, it's not a real issue to him, at least not yet.

His rite of passage body paint should keep most of anything spiritually off him, maybe somewhat physical too.

These things he didn't think often about and so he stopped thinking about it. Changing his set of thoughts towards camping. He could press on, but this was a nifty spot, good enough against the wind, and covered.

So he opted to set up camp tonight and start early in the morning for his final stop this winter.

With this in mind he started setting up camp when he stepped out of his small outcove to grab some water he paused.

Across the creek on a small low rise hill was a large dog just sitting there and giving him a thousand yard stare. Gazed at him with a quiet curious gaze.

He shifted as he noticed the odd behavior. It's the same dog he saw back in the mountain burial ground. At the time he felt his rite of passage heating up under the stare.

But now it felt cool like it had before after a few moments. Was this a spirit? Did it test his defense?

There is certainly a chance, one he couldn't place and one he decided to keep an eye on. Respectably, the dog kept its distance. So he decided that too would be his stance. Be respectful and keep a good distance, it could be said he isn't entirely knowledgeable.

Outlaw knew stuff, but not everything and frankly this? He felt he should know, but is lacking of that information. Perhaps he will ask his friends when he arrives. It's a two day walk, he would also ask them about his dreams.

About the whispering nightmares; he felt they too could help him. It has been touching on his stress with a creeping encroach. He felt horrible, like something happened.. or was going to happen, It felt bad, terribly bad. What's worse he felt like he was missing something important something painfully obvious.

He signed filling his water skins and returning to the fox fire within the outcove to treat the water.

Many question, many need answering and he only hoped to find them, or another to help find them. all In due time he assumed. For that's all he could conjure to hope for.

The night passed, cold but not so to be quite of great discomfort.

In the morning he checked to see if the odd dog was there, he was not. The spot it was in is now vacant. He could only feel relief? Or was it a new nerve. The worse is not seeing it, that creeping feeling of being watched sent a searing chill down his spine. He felt the paranoia working on his nerves.

Two days left.. wait one, today would be the second.

He burried the small pit and hoisted his bag onto his shoulders.

Stepping out of the outcove he felt a tinge of pain, his rite of passage body paint flicked with heat. He never found the source, looking around quietly.

Something felt off, sinister. The quietness never helped, because it shouldn't be this quiet. He signed in resignation and moved along quickly, peace sometimes came with danger. He had accepted this last night, but now he did not wish to stick around to find what was bothering him.

So he moved on quickly, crossing river creek and making his way along the rocky bases of the cliffs towards the wider forest.

It took a little while, but he heard the livened sounds of animals and birds. The sway of trees, the whisper of wind and the cricking of crickets.

He had paused for a moment, that sense of danger had ebbed and eventually all, but waned until it vanished without a trace.

He truly felt himself relax, realizing that even when he thought he relaxed around river creek. That he clearly had not, but now? He truely had.

Outlaw took a moment to enjoy this, that reprieve. In a place so far from home. A place that held a softer edge than what he is used to.

When moments passed and he felt that soothing breeze. He smiled to himself and moved along, perhaps the days ahead will be carefree as it feels now.

His friends would welcome him and he could talk his mind to them. The few that listened and knew a thing or two he did not.

With a happier mood he picked up the pace. Feeling that tonight just before the last day of his trek that he would be brewing some tea. For the last day he had not, not even feeling remotely safe to do so. Now he could, perhaps it will calm him further.

Happier days are ahead, this much he felt should be true. But there was a searing sting in the instincts. So infastasmly slight he did not pick up on it.

The trek was a beautifully kind moment, seeing the birds play in the canopy the squirrels racing along the brush and the occasional croaking near the creeks edge he traversed.

This is why he enjoyed the outdoors compared to the city. Something of this experience was oddly right, relaxed and peaceful.

This is how it should always be, he felt at peace here and opted to slow his pace to an almost crawl to enjoy it. Though in the midst of his travel he wrinkled his nose, picking up the slightest tinge of smoke. He sniffled and looked around, seeing no trail of smoke, no signs of flame. He decided to quickly scope off the path, but found nothing to note.

Strange he could have sworn he smelled the burn of wood. The charcoal smoking, he supposed he was just having one of those burnt toast moments.

However most concerning now was what he found hidden away just beyond the beaten path. The almost rotted clean corpse of a bear. It shared the same claw marks where it's skin lay tattered but he saw no signs of it being feasted on.

He had assumed the tree marks was from a bear, but if that was the case why was it here?

He felt a chill, those markings were not bear claws. Without a word he quickly got back onto the road and kept traveling.

Perhaps it's not best to think about it, after all isn't it taboo?

Ah who is he kidding? He deals with them at home. This is likely another of the folklore. Not a skinwalker either, a much worse sort. But he wasn't sure their name so he opted to assume them skinwalker, it's a bit bland and not right, this he knew.

But bland didn't mean bad, it kept things straight and true. He just had to assume it was a particularly scary one. Perhaps he hadn't seen it yet because of his rite of passage. Making him happy he prepared ahead of time.

This special protection has saved him alot. It's special due to the acknowledgement and blessing of sorts from the spirits of the forest and that one skinwalker.

A powerful protection indeed. Just then he crested a hill, ahead was another hill, he was so close. To quantify.. it should either be over that next hill or over the next three hills.

His destination was ahead.

Chapter 16

Peace and enjoyment of the forest and plains. Pointing towards just the horizon. That's where he is headed. Wrinkles his nose as he smells the lingers of smoke must be a large fire, likely a celebration bonfire?

He notices a recent encampment. Large one to maybe two dozen? He found five burnt campfires barely covered by dirt and recent signs of wear for horses and even a tinge of gunpowder. He frowns but doesn't find anything too out of place aside from a sloppy buried campfire.

Outlaw also assumes this Is where he got that smoke smell. Yet the fires appear at least a day old.. so he isn't sure.

He sets up camp a few miles from the one he found judging he would arrive near the later part of the day.

He had a restless night and awoke less than happy, he felt that same creeping foreboding, He wasn't sure why, but packed up nonetheless.

When he started his journey for it's final strafe. He found his stomach cramped and his body ached with an unseen pain he did not entirely figure out. It was a slow sobbing pain. The kind that builds and twist at the gut.

He picked up his pace, quickening his steps. The feeling only persisted forcing Him to stop and let it subside. Did he get sick? There was a chance. He then recalled, he forgot to brew that tea. Perhaps it would help.

So outlaw would find a spot build a small fire and listen to the forestry of animals as he set up, boiling the tea.

He noticed with a frown the forest felt foreboding and held a creeping sear. When he attuned to it. The lively sounds seemed so distant. but not in a dangerous way.. it felt.. sorrow?

He squinted his eyes as he taste the bitter tea. There it was again. The smell, smell of cinders and ash. The smell of smoke, something else too.. sinister and distinct. When Outlaw realized what the smell was he jumped to his feet, poured water on his small fire and covered it in dirt. Then he burst out of his rest spot and bolted, when the canopy broke he slid to a stop.

lazy exhausted pillars of smoke rose in curls from the direction he was traveling, black and ashened. The village!

Outlaw ran back to grab his backpack and then rushed out. It would be half a days walk, but he had thrown the notion of being leasure.

As he ran flash backs curled in the black smoke, he heard sounded a dissonance, broken and fragmented. He heard the thunder, small, large and different, he felt the singe of fire and the lingers of gunpowder residue.

At last when he crested a small hill Outlaw paused, his breath ragged, hitched in that moment for ahead where houses had been and gatherings would have taken place was misted by the grey's of smoke and the lazy almost exhausted pillars that clouded the skies with falling ash.

From this view alone he saw damages To buildings that were clearly battle damages.

Outlaw felt the tinge of searing heat return the twist in the gut hooked. For what he felt as the forest did..

Was sorrow as well.

Chapter 17

He pulled his rifle free, made sure he had loaded it and threw himself into a jog nearing the village. It's difficult to say if they ever named this place. Outlaw had never asked and never been told.

Let's call it Tu Village, for easier reference.

Tu Village was a small tribe, roughly a few hundred natives. They had sensible tabooes that never seemed too extreme or too lax like the others he had encountered. The spirits here were kind and firm. Like silk wrapping iron.

It did have warriors, and these are the first bodies he saw. Near its front he found a charred hut, sat against apart of charred wall, a native slouched and riddled with holes. He saw other bodies those hit before they could reach others not worth looking at.. the unlucky few hit by cannonballs.. its.. It was horrible.

Just seeing it made his legs tremble. He had seen death, but.. there was a difference when it was a people you knew for a long time. Though Outlaw was a loner in his own dwellings and traveled each year, he outta almost be apart of this tribe alone with how close he was to the people of Tu Village.

So it hurt to see this outcome to be helpless to it. His dreams echoed, hearing the echoes of battle that lingered here, he couldnt help but see his dream overlay Tu Villages fight. Screams and shouts, warriors rushing ahead to take cover whilst others help evacuate and defend those who cannot fight.

He twisted and turned his head to see the shadows of smoke screaming as gunfire roared twisted shadows rushing into the village.

The dreams echo faded leaving him weak in the knees as his emotions built, his grief delayed.

He held out hope that someone survived so he made his way through feeling a growing pain as he saw bodies of not just warriors but young and old, of women and even more heart wrenching children caught in the crossfire.

Who would do this? Why would they do this? Was it another tribe? Why couldn't he just go faster, perhaps if he got here in time he could have helped.. could have...

Outlaw paused, he felt a sear rise on his ritual of passage body paint. But this time he was far from weary, for his frayed nerves were thinning.

He found that same dog staring at him closer to the middle of the ruins. It turned away and walked a few paces, glancing back.

Outlaw blinked, it wanted him to follow?

Outlaw without hesitation did just that, keeping a respectful distance, if only just. He knew this dog was nothing normal, it followed him from a respectful distance and though his rite of passage kept heating up near it. He could only assume that is due to the forces behind the acknowledgement.

To remind, the ritual he had done in his cabin and been acknowledged by a forest spirit and skinwalker. This sort of protection was special because of that acknowledgement. So far this dog had not caused any damage and instead watched from afar, now it was leading him. Like a guide, they left Tu Village and walked for a time. When he saw the deeply hidden shelter where they would evacuate their people.

His heart sank, for the first thing he smelled was copper, and the stink of burnt flesh.

The dog stopped and stepped to the side, this is what it wanted him to see.

He turned his attention to the shelter it's door hanging loosely, outside were several dead figures but he didn't seem to see them, so focused on what was within to see the bodies of those whom caused this terrible event.

His hesitanting approach, each step a mountain of pressure and sorrow weighing on him. The gradual horror on his face growing as he saw more into the shelter..

They had been slaughtered, this was a shelter for the woman and children, for the old and the sick.

It now came to be their tomb, burnt bodies littering within. Charred wood of sticks and straw..

Outlaw fell to his knees when he recognized a partially charred body, a friend of his. Their face held a touch of indignation and fear.

He dropped his rifle as Outlaw found himself broken, crying for the dead and their sorrow. That's when he saw the bodies.. of the enemy, bluish uniforms. The US army, Outlaw remembered now.

He recalled a group of riders a week or so before, gathering at the town. These appeared to be the same, their connected. And his dream, the helpless feeling of being unable to warn them in time, being too late, watching a massacre that plagued his mind. He did not think this could happen.

Why couldn't he get here in time?!

Outlaw renewed in his vigor and cried harder.

Drawn into a long drawn wail, and with each tear that sorrow stirred deeper feelings. The trees around him seemed to curl in, whispers grew trying to sooth him. Through teary eyes he saw echoes of shadows loom, kneeling near him. One of them reaching out.

He blinked and the shadows seemed to vanish.

When he turned the dog was gone, but in its place the quiet lingers of smoke and a slow emotion that quieted him within hours.

There was a strange ire, it prickled at his skin. A rage that wasn't his but also his. His rite of passage felt like ice on the skin. A breeze catch the trees, they swayed into a stillness that was unnatural.

He turned back to his friend and noticed the facial expression.

Rage.

Chapter 18

Outlaw worked for days, a grueling work to gather up the bodies into a bonfire pit. He decided after conducting true burial to the best of his abilities that he would decide what to do.

He couldn't deny it, he too felt great rags. These actions even if the US army did them were particularly heinous. He felt they were more so wrong than they should have been.

Outlaw had to stop many times, battling an onset of intense grief and depression. The only thing helping him was the dog would appear sometimes, that or brewing up tea and trying to listen in on the spiritual world.

It took outlaw four days to gather them all, alot of it was recovering, gaging and taking breaks to not crack under his own emotions.

Through will and some methods of calming and guidance he managed.

He had also spent this time for wood collection and preparing the pit so to manage a heat strong enough to cremate.

And he did just that, when he lit the bonfire and quietly watched the fires. He vowed to himself and to them.

"I do not care what I must do or how far I must fall, I swear on you and all of those within Tu Village.. that I, Outlaw will avenge you, be I successful or not, I will truly try my best." He vowed to the pillared flames, where ashes arose and swirled.

The spiritual world took this vow to heart and he heard the agitated spirits wholeheartedly agree. He also saw other spirit walkers a distance from here tremble.

The way Outlaw had put it..

'I do not care' 'or how far I must fall'

These were significant and no walker missed the vow, nor the strength of its truth. So the forest shadow is enraged? What did they do? And who did it?

Outlaw opened his eyes and sobbed where he had stood watching the flames for a long time.

The day passed to night and it was hard to tell what his rite of passage reacted to, from the start to end of his vow and up to now he was numb to the searing chill and the chilling heat.

He found that dog next to him. Sitting close and watching the fire. He glanced at them and asked outright, a surefire taboo. But he couldn't care.

"Are you a skinwalker?"

The dog looked at him, it's eyes beady and held intelligence. Of course it wouldn't answer and in general the fact it didn't react aggressively to his blatant ask was interesting.

No, it reacted to his next question.

"is there a way to gather more of you?"

It blinked at him, why would he.. want that? It seemed to ask in a silent stare.

Outlaw smiled and stared into the dancing flames.

"I want to show them the true horrors of the land, for just as we respect you, and you, the spirits respect us. So when your harmed we find it tabooed and not right, but when we are harmed. It's you who grow angered.. right?"

He stated without looking, it wasn't a question, even if it was posed as one.

When he looked at the dog, to his expectation it was gone. He only hoped it understood his meaning, now whatever happened after this point was up in the wind.

Outlaw felt he might not come out of this unscathed, perhaps he would die. But there was something within that told him he would die In a different way. Though he wasn't entirely sure what that feeling was.

He had managed to do hold his grief, though it grew delayed again. He knew one day he would have to confront it.

Grief was a terrible thing, it stuck around and only time could heal it. He felt many days of dreary dreams and tears are ahead, like a trail of tears.

He wiped the tears that he shed at the final hour of the waning blaze.

Outlaw slowly got up, looking into the fires and only smiling as he waved his hands.

"I'll see you, next year."

He said as he stepped back, Grabbing his backpack, Outlaw hoisted it onto his shoulders and back. Turning away he paused, then glanced back.

"Rest in peace, and know that I will shed blood in your place. Goodbye."

Outlaw walked away, not seeing the wisping shadows that watched him go they begun to trail behind slipping into his shadow as Outlaw left Tu village.

Changed he was, blood he would soon shed.

End Of Book One

About the Author

Howdy, Author here. Names Bobbydale Murr. I'm 23 years old and iv been a long time author or attempts of it. I have alot of books, but never finished anything aside from two. One of which your reading, Just a little about me, I am Texan, iv lived in Texas all my life. I have some native family and what not, I have a love for writing and gaming amongst other things. I do hope you enjoy my works, it's been trial and error for a time and this looks like a real shot somewhere, anyway that's enough about me. As you can see first time writing one of these.

Milton Keynes UK
Ingram Content Group UK Ltd.
UKHW030147051224
452010UK00001B/60

9 798230 915140